LUCY DANIELS

Ashleigh McGregor

The Proud Piglet

Hodder
Children's
Books

A division of Hachette Children's Books

To Betty Elwell – who loves all things piggy!

Special thanks to Narinder Dhami

Little Animal Ark is a trademark of Working Partners Limited
Text copyright © 2002 Working Partners Limited
Created by Working Partners Limited, London, W6 0QT
Illustrations copyright © 2002 Andy Ellis

This edition published in 2007

First published in Great Britain in 2002 by Hodder Children's Books

The rights of Lucy Daniels and Andy Ellis to be identified as the author
and illustrator of this work respectively have been asserted by them in
accordance with the Copyright, Designs and Patents Act 1988.

2

A Catalogue record for this book is available from the
British Library

ISBN-13: 978 0 340 9359 9

Printed and bound in Great Britain by
Clays Ltd, St Ives plc

Hodder Children's Books
A division of Hachette Children's Books
338 Euston Road, London NW1 3BH
An Hachette Livre UK Company

Chapter One

"I think I'm going to melt, Grandad!" Mandy Hope said. "It's so *hot*." She looked up at the blue sky. It was the first week of the summer holidays, and it felt like the sun had been shining for ever.

Grandad Hope stopped digging and wiped his brow. "We'll be finished soon," he said. "There's not much more to do."

Mandy was helping her grandad to clear a patch of garden at Animal Ark, where she lived. Her mum and dad were very busy at work, and Grandad Hope loved gardening so he had offered to help out.

Just then Mandy's mum came out carrying her vet's bag.

"Mandy, I'm going to Appletree Cottage," she called. "Do you want to come with me?"

Mandy dropped her armful of weeds into the wheelbarrow and brushed the front of her T-shirt. Her mum had visited Appletree Cottage before. "That's where Mr and Mrs Henderson live," she said. "And they've got lots of animals."

"You'd better go with your Mum, then!" Grandad Hope laughed.

Mandy was mad about animals. Her mum and dad were both vets. There were always lots of animals around, and that was just the way Mandy liked it.

"Are you sure you don't mind, Grandad?" Mandy asked.

Grandad Hope shook his head. "No, of course not," he said. "Off you go, love."

"Don't work too hard," Mandy's mum said to Grandad. "It's much too hot."

Grandad smiled and nodded. "But I like digging!" he said. He picked up his spade again. "See you later."

Mrs Hope and Mandy went out to the car.

"Why are we going to Appletree Cottage, Mum?" Mandy asked. "Is one of the animals sick?"

"No," replied her mum. "The Hendersons have gone on holiday, and someone else is looking after the animals. Mrs Henderson asked if I would visit to see if they need any advice."

"Who is looking after the animals?" Mandy wanted to know.

"Mr Henderson's sister, Mrs Ford," said Mrs Hope. "And her children, Emma and Ellie."

Mandy looked out of the window as her mum drove through Welford. They went past Lilac Cottage, where Mandy's gran and grandad lived. Then they came to Appletree Cottage, right on the edge of the village.

Mrs Hope knocked on the door of the cottage. It was opened by a little girl. Another girl was standing beside her. She looked about the same age as Mandy. Behind them stood a tall lady.

"Hello," said the lady. "I'm Claire Ford." She smiled down at the little girl. "This is Ellie. And that's her big sister Emma. You must be Mrs Hope and Mandy."

"That's right," said Mrs Hope. "It's very nice to meet you."

"Hello," Mandy said. She smiled at Emma and Ellie.

"Have you come to see our animals?" Ellie asked shyly.

"Well, they're not really ours!" said Emma, squeezing past her sister. "We're just looking after them."

"I can't wait to see them," Mandy said.

"I'm going to stay here for a minute and talk to Claire," said Emily Hope.

"Come on then, Mandy, I'll show you round," said Emma. She grabbed Mandy's hand and took her into the back garden.

Mandy's eyes opened very wide. "What a lot of animals!" she cried. The garden was very big. And there were animals *everywhere*!

In the middle of the lawn was a duck-pond. Snowy white ducks were swimming on the water, quacking loudly. There was an orchard on the other side of the garden. Mandy counted eight sheep grazing under the trees.

In a small field at the bottom of the garden, a Jersey cow was looking over the gate. She stared at Mandy with her big brown eyes.

"Her name's Dolly," Emma told Mandy.

They ran across the lawn to say hello to Dolly. They had to run in a big circle to dodge a sprinkler which was squirting water over the grass.

As they reached the fence, Mandy jumped in surprise. Something was moving under the hedge at the side of the field. Something pink.

Suddenly, it shot out and dashed towards the gate, squealing loudly.

"Oh!" Mandy gasped. "It's a piglet!"

Chapter Two

The piglet pushed her little pink
snout through the bars of the gate.

"This is Rosy," Emma
laughed. "Isn't she cute?"

"Yes, she is," Mandy agreed.
She thought Rosy was a very good
name. The piglet was a lovely
rosy-pink colour.

"She's very friendly," Emma
went on. She pushed open the
gate, and they went into the field.

"Say hello to Mandy, Rosy!"

Rosy trotted over to Mandy and began to sniff her shoes.

"Hello, Rosy," Mandy said. She bent down and patted the piglet's back. Rosy gave a squeaky grunt, as if she was saying hello too.

"My auntie and uncle haven't had Rosy for very long," said Emma. She closed the gate behind them. "She's only five weeks old."

Mandy watched as Rosy began to snuffle around in the grass. "Is she hungry?" she asked. She put her hand in her pocket. "I've got some mints. Can she have one?"

"No, Rosy can't have any of our food because she's only a baby," Emma explained. "She has special pignuts. And she shares Dolly's drinking trough, over there." She pointed to a metal trough in the corner of the field.

"Does Rosy like living in the field with Dolly?" Mandy asked.

"Oh, yes," replied Emma. "But she loves playing with us, too. Look!" She turned and ran off across the field.

Rosy gave a loud squeal and galloped after her, pink ears flapping madly.

Mandy couldn't stop laughing as she followed them. The piglet was just like a little dog!

Emma lay down, and so did Rosy. She flopped on to the warm grass and waved her trotters in the air.

"Isn't she great?" Emma said proudly.

Mandy nodded. "I think she's really funny!" she said. And she tickled Rosy's tummy.

Just then, Mandy's mum walked down the garden with Mrs Ford and Ellie.

Mandy waved. "Mum, come and meet Rosy," she called.

Rosy jumped up and raced over to the gate. She seemed to like having visitors!

"Hello, Rosy," said Mrs Hope. She scratched Rosy's ears through the bars of the fence.

"Don't let Rosy out yet,"
Mrs Ford said, as Emma opened
the gate. "She can come into
the garden later, when it's her
teatime."

Rosy looked rather sad when
Mandy and Emma left the field.
She grunted crossly as they
walked up the garden.

Mrs Hope looked at her watch. "Mandy, it's time for us to go," she said. "I've got some more calls to make."

Mandy felt disappointed. She wanted to stay a bit longer to see Rosy being fed.

"Mum, can Mandy stay and play with us?" asked Emma. "Ellie and I were going to run under the sprinkler to cool down."

"Oh, can I, Mum?" Mandy asked. "Please?"

Mandy's mum looked at Mrs Ford, who smiled and nodded.

"I'll pick you up when I've finished my calls then, Mandy," said Mrs Hope. "See you later."

"Bye, Mum," Mandy said, giving her a kiss.

"I'm glad you're staying," said Emma. "You can help us feed Rosy later."

"Thanks," Mandy said happily. She was looking forward to that already!

"Come on," said Emma. "Let's play under the sprinkler first. I'll lend you a swimsuit."

"OK," Mandy said. "Look out!"

Mandy and Emma both jumped as a shower of water shot towards them. Ellie had turned on the hose and was aiming it right at them. She ran away laughing as Mandy and Emma got wet.

"You wait, Ellie!" said Emma with a grin. She quickly filled a bucket of water under the tap, and then ran after her sister. "I'm going to get you!" she shouted.

Mandy laughed as Emma chased Ellie down the garden.

Emma caught up with her
and threw the bucket of water
over Ellie. So Ellie ran to get her
water pistol. She filled it up and
began squirting water at Mandy
and Emma. They both ran
round the garden, trying
to dodge her.

"I can see you three are
having a great time," Mrs Ford

said with a smile. She was sitting on the patio, reading a book. "But I think it's time for Rosy's dinner. Emma, will you go and fetch her?"

"OK, Mum," said Emma. "Do you want to come with me, Mandy?"

"Yes, please," Mandy said. She hurried down the garden after Emma.

Rosy was lying under a shady tree, keeping out of the sun. As soon as she saw Mandy and Emma she jumped up and trotted over to the gate, squealing noisily.

"She knows it's time for her dinner!" said Emma. "Let's open the gate, Mandy."

"Do we have to pick her up and carry her?" Mandy asked.

Emma shook her head. "Oh no," she said. "Rosy's very well-behaved. She'll just follow us into the garden."

Emma unlocked the gate and Mandy pushed it open.

Rosy raced through like a little pink rocket and ran up the garden as fast as she could.

"Rosy!" yelled Emma. "Come back!"

Chapter Three

Mandy and Emma dashed after Rosy. Ellie and Mrs Ford were on the patio, staring open-mouthed at the runaway piglet.

"She's never done this before!" panted Emma. "Where's she going?"

"It looks like she's heading for the duck-pond," Mandy gasped.

She was right. Rosy *was* making

for the duck-pond. *Splash!* With a
loud oink, the piglet jumped
straight into the water.

The ducks quacked crossly as
Rosy dived in. They flapped their
wings and flew
out of the way.

Rosy didn't seem to care. She splashed around in the water, churning up the bottom of the pond with her tiny hooves.

Soon the water was all muddy. But Rosy looked as if she was really enjoying herself.

"We'd better get her out of there," said Emma.

Mandy nodded. It wasn't just the water that was dirty. Rosy was too!

Mrs Ford came over. She looked a bit worried. "Is Rosy all right?" she asked.

"I think so," Mandy said. "The water isn't very deep."

The ducks were still flapping

around, quacking loudly.
They didn't like having a pig
in their pond!

"Don't worry, Mum," said
Emma. "We'll get Rosy out."

Mandy and Emma waded
into the duck-pond. It was very
muddy round the edges, and
their feet and legs got very dirty.

Rosy was enjoying herself too much to take any notice of them. She kept on splashing about, spraying Mandy and Emma with brown water.

"Be careful, girls," said Mrs Ford.

Mandy was closest to Rosy. She leaned over and wrapped her arms around the grubby little piglet.

Rosy wasn't very happy about leaving the duck-pond. She wriggled about, trying to get free. But Mandy held on tightly.

Emma helped Mandy to carry Rosy out of the pond and put her on the grass.

Mandy and Emma looked down at themselves. They were covered in mud. And so was Rosy. You could hardly see that she was pink at all!

Chapter Four

Mrs Ford shook her head. "Look at you!" she said. "Oh, Rosy! You've scared the ducks, and now the girls are all dirty too."

"I don't think we can call you Rosy anymore," giggled Ellie. "We'd better call you Muddy instead!"

Rosy snorted loudly. Her mouth looked all smiley, as if she was laughing.

"Shall I get the hose, Mum?" asked Emma. "Then we can wash Rosy – and us too!"

"Good idea," said Mrs Ford.

Mandy nodded. She didn't mind getting muddy. It was often tricky to keep clean around animals. But now the mud was starting to dry in the hot sunshine, and it made her skin feel very itchy.

She kept hold of Rosy while Emma ran to get the hose. Emma pointed the end at Mandy and Rosy. "Here goes!" she shouted.

Ellie turned on the tap and water came gushing out.

Mandy got down on her knees and began to rub the mud off Rosy. The water ran off her skin in brown trickles.

Rosy wriggled a bit, but she didn't seem to mind too much. "Good girl, Rosy," Mandy said. "You'll soon be all pink again."

Just then, Mrs Hope returned. "Hello, everyone," she said. "I've finished my calls." Then she spotted Mandy, Emma and Rosy. "What have you three been doing?" she gasped.

"Rosy jumped into the duck-pond, Mum," Mandy said, grinning. "And she got all muddy. So now we're cleaning her up."

"And we're washing ourselves too, Mrs Hope," added Emma.

"Poor Rosy," said Mrs Hope.

"She must have been feeling rather warm. Pigs hate being too hot."

"So she jumped into the pond to get cool, and got all muddy as well," laughed Emma. "Never mind, Rosy. You'll soon be nice and clean again." She sprayed some more water over the piglet.

Mandy wiped the last bit of mud from Rosy's ears. Now she was rosy-pink again.

"Well, Rosy actually meant to get herself muddy," said Mrs Hope.

Everyone looked at her.

"What do you mean, Mum?" Mandy asked.

"Pigs love mud," Mrs Hope explained. "They use it to keep themselves clean and comfortable."

Mandy felt very puzzled. That didn't make sense!

But Rosy grunted, as if she agreed with Mandy's mum.

"Pigs roll in mud, then they get out and let the mud dry," Mrs Hope went on. "The mud traps any nasty fleas or insects on their skin. Then the pigs scratch off the mud *and* the bugs by rubbing themselves against a tree or a fence."

"But Rosy can't do that now," said Emma. She looked worried. "We've already washed her."

"Never mind," said Mrs Hope. "Rosy will get another chance to roll in the mud, I'm sure!"

They all looked at Rosy, who was snuffling around in the grass.

Mandy felt sorry for the little piglet. All Rosy had wanted to do was cool off and get herself clean, just like a grown-up pig.

"I expect she's hungry now," said Mrs Ford. "Emma, would you and Mandy like to get her pig-nuts? Ellie and I will keep an eye on Rosy."

"OK, Mum," said Emma.

Mandy followed Emma to the shed where the pig-nuts were kept. "It's a shame for Rosy, isn't it?" she said. "She must have been feeling really hot if she wanted to jump into the pond."

"We'll have to try and keep her cool from now on," said Emma. "We can let her play under the sprinkler with us."

"But she still won't be able to get muddy like a proper pig, will she?" Mandy said. "And I don't think the ducks like sharing their pond with her!"

"What should we do then?" asked Emma.

Mandy shook her head.

"I don't know," she sighed.
She looked at the ducks,
bobbing happily on their pond.

And then she had a brilliant idea.
"Emma," she said, "wouldn't it be
great if Rosy had a muddy place
all of her own?"

Chapter Five

"Mum, Mandy's had a really good idea!" said Emma. She put down the bowl of pig-nuts in front of Rosy. The piglet pushed her pink nose into the bowl and began to eat.

"What is it?" asked Mrs Ford.

"Well, I thought it might be nice if Rosy had her own pond," Mandy said. "Then she wouldn't try to jump into the duck-pond when it's hot."

"That *does* sound like a good idea," said Mrs Ford. She looked at Mandy's mum. "What do you think?" she asked.

"I think Rosy would love it," Mrs Hope said with a smile.

"Who's going to dig it, though?" said Mrs Ford. "It would be quite a big job. And I can't do it. I have a bad back."

"Maybe Uncle Rob and Auntie Jen can do it," said Emma. "When they get home from their holiday."

Her mum nodded. "Yes, I think that's the best thing," she said.

Mandy tickled Rosy's ears.

"Did you hear that, Rosy?" she whispered. "You're going to have your very own pond!"

It was time for Mandy and Mrs Hope to go home. So they said goodbye to the Fords, and to Rosy, and set off in the Land-rover.

"It's a shame Rosy has to wait for her paddling-pool until Mr and Mrs Henderson get back," Mandy sighed. "I just hope it's not too hot tomorrow."

When they got home to Animal Ark, Mandy went into the garden to see how Grandad was getting on. She took him a big glass of orange squash.

Grandad Hope was leaning on his spade. He smiled at Mandy. "Is that for me?" he asked.

Mandy nodded and gave him the glass.

He took a long drink. "Thanks, love. That was thirsty work!" he said.

Mandy looked at all the digging Grandad Hope had done that afternoon. "Grandad, you like digging, don't you?" she said.

Her grandad grinned. "You know I do!" he said. "Now, what are you up to, Mandy Hope?"

Mandy told him all about Rosy, and how she really needed her own pond right away. "Do you think you could dig a pond for Rosy?" she asked.

Grandad Hope beamed and put his arm round Mandy. "Of course I could!" he said.

Chapter Six

"We're nearly there," Grandad Hope puffed. He lifted up another spadeful of earth. "Do you think this will be deep enough?"

"Oh, yes," Mandy said. "It's nearly as deep as the duck-pond!"

It was another very sunny day. Grandad Hope was digging the pond in Rosy's field. Mandy, Emma and Ellie were watching him. It was so hot, they were all wearing swimsuits.

Rosy was lying under the tree, watching Grandad too. She blinked at him with her little black eyes. She looked a bit puzzled, as if she couldn't work out what was going on.

"I think that's it," Grandad Hope said with a smile, sticking his spade into the ground. "Time to fill it with water."

Mandy and Emma dragged the hose across the grass until it reached the hole that Grandad had dug. Ellie ran up the garden to turn on the tap.

Soon water came bubbling out of the hose, and began to fill the hole. Mandy and Emma cheered.

"Thanks, Grandad," Mandy said, giving him a big hug.

Rosy sat up. She looked at the water splashing into the big hole. With a squeal of delight,

she rushed across the field and
dived straight into her new pond!

"Rosy, wait!" called Ellie.
"We haven't filled it up yet."

But Rosy didn't seem to
mind. She splashed and paddled
in the muddy water, grunting
happily.

"Look, Grandad," Mandy said. "Rosy loves it."

"Why don't you join her?" said Grandad. "It looks like she's found the best way to cool off!"

So Mandy, Emma and Ellie jumped into the pond too.

SPLASH!

Rosy didn't mind sharing at all. There was plenty of room for everybody. Soon the four of them were covered in mud from head to toe.

Mrs Ford heard the shouting and came to see what was going on. "Tea's ready," she called with a smile. "But I think you'd better clean yourselves up first."

Mandy, Emma and Ellie waded out of the pond.

Rosy splashed out after them, then trotted off to lie down in the sun.

"I wonder if Rosy knows how to give herself a proper piggy cleaning now?" Mandy said.

"When all that mud's dry, maybe she'll scrape it off, like Mum said."

Emma frowned. "I don't know if she knows what to do," she said. "Do you think we should show her?"

"Don't worry," said Grandad Hope. "Rosy seems a very clever piglet. I'm sure she'll work it out."

"I hope so," Mandy said. She looked at Rosy. The piglet's little pink ears twitched as she snoozed.

"I don't think *we'd* better try scraping our mud off!" said Emma. She picked up the hose. "I'll help you two clean up!" And she squirted a jet of water at Mandy and Ellie.

The water sparkled like glass in the sun, and felt icy-cold on Mandy's skin.

Ellie laughed, then grabbed the hose from Emma and aimed it at her.

When they were all clean, Ellie turned off the hose, and Mandy and Emma dragged it back out of the field.

Mrs Ford waved to them from the patio. She had made a big jug of orange squash. And Mandy's gran had sent some of her home-made scones. Grandad Hope was already tucking in!

"Come on, Emma," Mandy said. "I'm starving!"

"Let's go and see if Rosy's cleaned herself yet," Mandy said after tea.

Emma and Ellie nodded. They jumped to their feet and ran down the garden.

Rosy was standing next to the tree. She grunted loudly as she rubbed her muddy body against the trunk. All the dry mud was peeling off, and Rosy was slowly turning pink again.

"Clever girl, Rosy!" Mandy called.

Rosy scraped off the last bit of mud. She looked down at her pink body and shook herself. With her head held high, she trotted over to the gate and pushed her snout through the bars.

Mandy reached down and patted her head. "You look really proud of yourself, Rosy," she laughed. "You know you're a proper pig now, don't you!"

Chapter One

"Come on, Ben!" called Mandy Hope. "Haven't you finished yet?"

It was lunchtime at Welford Primary School. Mandy went over to the table where her friend Ben Stokes was still eating his sandwiches.

"I don't know how you ate your lunch so fast," said Ben.

"It's because I'm so excited!" Mandy told him with a grin.

"I can't *wait* to see Scott's hamsters!"

Scott was Ben's big brother. He was in Class 6, which had a Pet of the Week lesson every Friday. Someone was allowed to bring their pet to school for the whole class to see. And this afternoon Scott was bringing his hamster, Scrabble, with three of her babies!

"I'm excited too," said Ben, munching on his last sandwich. "Even though I see them every day."

"Lucky you!" Mandy said. Mandy *loved* animals – which was good, because there were always lots of them at home in Animal Ark. Her mum and dad were vets.

Mandy didn't have a pet of her own, but she didn't mind too much – she often got the chance to play with her friends' pets.

At last, Ben finished his lunch. He stood up and smoothed down his spiky hair with his hand.

Mandy grinned. Ben was *always* doing that, because his hair was *always* sticking up!